JJ

Sti   Stimson, Joan

         Swim polar bear,
         swim!

Swim Polar Bear, Swim!

Swim
Polar Bear,
Swim!

Joan Stimson

Illustrated by
Meg Rutherford

Look out for *Big Panda, Little Panda* and
A New Home for Tiger, also by
Joan Stimson and Meg Rutherford.

First edition for the United States and Canada
published 1996 by Barron's Educational Series, Inc.

© Copyright 1996 by Joan Stimson (text)
© Copyright 1996 by Meg Rutherford (illustrations)

First published by Scholastic Ltd,
London, England, 1996

All inquiries should be addressed to:
Barron's Educational Series, Inc.
250 Wireless Boulevard
Hauppauge, New York 11788

Library of Congress Catalog Card No. 96-84162
International Standard Book No. 0-8120-6634-0 (hardcover)
0-8120-9888-9 (paperback)

PRINTED IN HONG KONG
9 8 7 6 5 4 3 2 1

Polar Star was the brightest, liveliest bear cub in the
entire Arctic.

He could turn somersaults almost before he could crawl.

He *never* stopped asking questions.

And, at bedtime, after the first story, he wanted another ... and another.

Polar Moon found it hard to keep up. Sometimes she complained.

But at the end of the day she always said the same thing. "You are the most wonderful bear cub. And I am the proudest mother in the world!"

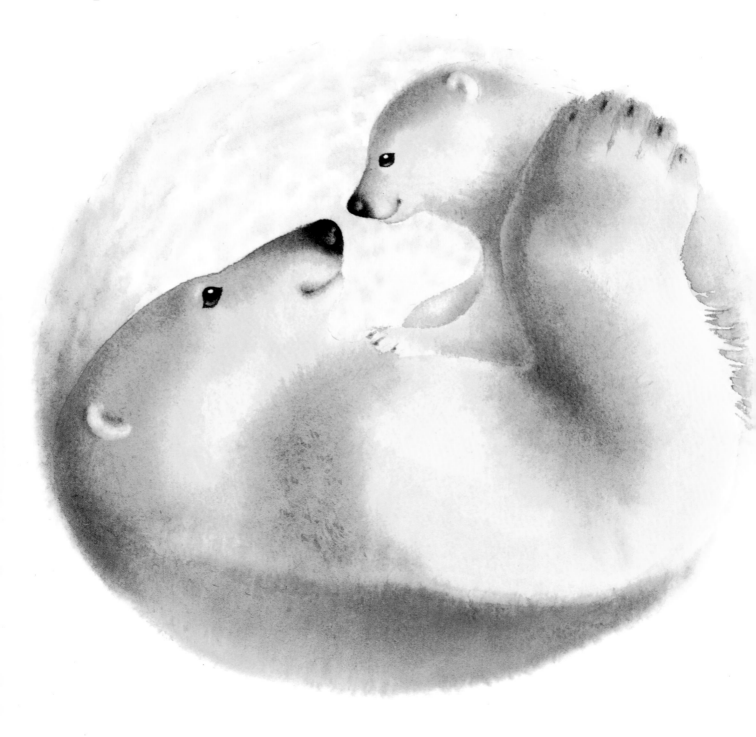

When spring came, Polar Moon led Polar Star down to the ocean.

"It's time for your first swimming lesson,"
she told him. Polar Star dipped his
paw in the water.

"Is it deep? Is it slippery? And what shall I do with my paws?" he asked.

"Jump up," said Polar Moon, "and I'll show you."

As soon as Polar Moon started to swim, Polar Star quivered with excitement.

"Can I try?" he asked. And without waiting for an answer, he slid down his mother's nose and into the water!

Polar Star gasped. Polar Star spluttered. And, although Mom scooped him up in no time at all, he felt sure he had swallowed the ocean.

"Never mind," said Polar Moon at bedtime. "You are still a wonderful bear cub. Now, let's have a story and we can try again tomorrow."

The next day Polar Star didn't feel so brave. He clung to his mother until her fur hurt.

And, when at last he allowed himself to be lowered into the water, he flapped and floundered.

"My paws keep sinking," he wailed. And he hung on even tighter.

"You are a wonderful bear cub," yawned Polar Moon at bedtime. "But how my back aches!"

Days passed and Polar Star grew more and more disappointed. He'd never found anything difficult before. And the more he worried about swimming, the more unhappy he felt in the water.

Mom was disappointed too. She wanted to help, but didn't know how. Then one night Polar Moon was so tired she spoke without thinking.
"Oh, Polar Star, I do wish you could swim."

All through the dark Polar Star lay awake. He tried to remember the last time Mom had said she was proud of him.

And, when Polar Moon came in next morning, Polar Star
was buried ... under the bedclothes.
"Whatever's wrong?" asked Polar Moon.

For a long time there was no reply. But at last Polar Star
spoke up.
"If I don't learn how to swim today," he said in a muffled
voice, "will you still love me?"

Polar Moon pulled back the covers and held her cub. "Oh, Polar Star!" she cried. "It doesn't matter if you *never* learn to swim, I shall love you to the end of the ocean!"

Polar Star bounded out of bed with a somersault. All through breakfast he asked questions.

And later that morning Polar Star and Polar Moon slid gently into the water.

At first Polar Star held tightly to Mom's tail. But, as he remembered what she had told him, he relaxed and, without thinking, let go.

"Where are you?" cried Polar Moon in a panic. She dived deep to rescue him.
But Polar Star was nowhere to be found.

At last Polar Moon came to the surface.
"I'm *here*!" panted Polar Star in the distance.
"And my paws aren't sinking," he told her proudly.

Then, with a splash and a flash of silver, Polar Star gave a great whoop of delight.

"I'm swimming! I'm swimming!" he called.

And his cry seemed to echo to the end of the ocean.